DANCING WITH THE GHOSTS

Nancy McWhorter

ISBN: 9798798609741

DEDICATION

This story is dedicated to my Muse, who resides on a Louisiana Bayou

CONTENTS

NOTE FROM THE AUTHOR

ME: No, I still don’t.

YOU: You still don’t what?

ME: Believe in ghosts. But they do make for a lovely story!

FORWARD

ABOUT MY MUSE

My muse does live on a Louisiana bayou, takes tourists on swamp tours, feeds her pet alligators, drinks mint julips, and wears frothy, flowing dresses when she dances in front of her slightly rundown shack that sits at the very edge of the water. Alligators have been known to walk through her front door and spread their fat, flat bodies out on the worn carpet in front of her 28" TV that is always tuned in to National Geographic.

She visits occasionally and unexpectedly. I will awake in the night to find her sitting on the end of my bed, or in the case of her recent visit, she came to the Italian restaurant/bar where I like to go dancing. Suddenly, I smelled the scent of the bayou, had thoughts of Spanish moss hung trees, turtles sunning on logs, alligators cruising the edge of slow-moving water, and I sensed the aroma of mint and bourbon.

In the small dimly lit, dark paneled alcove of the bar, she was sitting alone at a table for two, looking extremely impatient. She was stunningly dressed in a frothy, turquoise handkerchief hemmed dress, colorful flowered leather boots (a fashion nod at being in Texas), and an amazing hand-crafted turquoise and alligator tooth necklace. Apparently, she had been visiting in Texas for a few months and decided she would never adjust to our ways. To her credit, she did catch the fashion look. I think the boots were too confining. She preferred bare feet.

Anyway, she informed me that she loathed Italian cuisine, and is leaving for home for some Cajun food, so I paid close attention to her vision for another book. She recommended that I continue the saga of Elizabeth Whites' life in *A Sack Lunch with the Ghosts*. And as I had ended it with that possibility, I took her advice.

So, here we go!

CHAPTER ONE
NEW BEGINNING

My name is Elizabeth White. Everyone calls me Libby. For the last two years I have been living in a small Texas town with my grandmother and grandfather.

I had found a summer job in an old book shop run by an elderly man named Lucus. And during that time, I discovered that there were ghosts living and working on the abandoned floor above. To my great sadness, as I had become very fond of them, they realized their condition and moved on, along with a sweet ghostly dress maker who owned a shop down the street.

On the day they left, a handsome man named John Shumaker walked into the store. He and Lucus had been negotiating by long distance the sale of the bookstore. Turns out he was a distant relative of Mrs. Shumaker, one the ghost's upstairs. His plan was to restore the building and turn it into a museum, which would bring revenue to our small Texas town, one that had been pushed to almost obscurity by a new interstate. Our only claim to existence was an off ramp and a small sign with the town name and distance to it. We did not even get one of those nice, colorful signs that list restaurants, gas stations, etc. Not that we had any of that, but we do have a Dairy Queen, the social hub of our small community. Seems like they could have mentioned that as someone might like some ice cream to break up a long drive on a monotonous highway.

But John had worked hard to change our town's circumstances and mine! The first day we met he practically proposed and I, in amusement, practically said yes.

And together with Lucas' and my input, we have restored the bookstore to the original Mercantile and the upstairs offices into a museum that boasts a lovely plaque with the names of past tenants;

Mrs. Shumaker – whose husband owned the building

Dr. Oldman – a young Dentist, shot by a jealous husband

Mr. Malcolm Smith – Lawyer

Miss Lucinda Avery – Photographer and fiancée to Mr. Smith

Mabel – town dress maker

I have been so happy with my inclusion in this project. And as of yesterday, I am now officially Mrs. Elizabeth Shumaker, wife, and partner in John's upcoming enterprises with the past.

We were married in the small white wood-sided Baptist Church on the edge of town. My beautiful vintage dress was conveniently found packed nicely in a trunk in the attic of the dress shop. Mabel's name tag was sewn in the neck and hand made with all the lace, pearls, and small buttons of the day. And John wore a handsome tuxedo in the style of the 1800's. It was our tribute to my ghostly friends.

The church was filled with sunflowers, as was my bouquet, to match the perfect sunny late spring day.

After the ceremony we all moved to the Dairy Queen for the reception. It had been transformed for the occasion with white table clothes, real China, vases of flowers, and boasted a high school string quartet that played lovely old tunes that we danced to.

My Grandmother and Grandfather were there, but not my parents as they were traveling in Morocco, living their passion for each other's lives that never quite included me. But it does not matter now, as I have my own true love into which I can immerse myself. Never in my wildest childhood dreams would I have believed I would find such happiness.

CHAPTER TWO
THE TRIP

John has decided (with my absolute approval) to spend our honeymoon on a road trip through some Southern towns, stopping to investigate historical sites with haunted stories attached. And to finally end up in New Orleans. I am extremely excited about the prospects for finding another small piece of history to delve into and renovate. The smell of old and musty is intoxicating for me.

Our first stop was Jefferson, Texas. A lovely historic town where we stayed in a Bed and Breakfast in a lovely room filled with antique furniture. Breakfast was divine, of course. If the food is any indication of what is to come, then I may be a divorcee by the end of the trip because I will definitely lose whatever shape I had that was attractive to John.

John's day was spent with realtors while I roamed the

town. Dinner was delightful and then we took a ghost tour. And yes, I saw plenty of them as I did in several towns and cities, especially New Orleans. So many ghosts and they knew I was aware of them and could see them, but I could tell they saw themselves as celebrities and acted as such by giving the human thrill- seekers a touch of cold, a moment of visibility, or an act of moving things around in a room. All extremely exciting, of course, but a game for them to amuse themselves as they wandered in their lostness.

Every historic town has its tragedies and consequential phenomenon that are turned into tourist attractions. I do not think that is John's ambition for his projects, at least I do not believe it is at this point. He wants to preserve places that have gone unnoticed but are historically important, like my little bookstore in a small Texas town. That there was another "life" to the place makes it more exciting to try and restore a building to its actual important era. If that makes any sense? So, we traveled on through the South with its charming ambience. Still looking for a special place to embrace and reveal its past soul.

New Orleans was a disappointment business wise, but we had a lovely time visiting the famous places and eating exquisite food. Antoine's was my favorite. Such a step back in time and the best bread pudding ever! I loved the

Two Sisters and was upset when our city tour guide touted the newer restaurants while disparaging the older ones that he felt had lost touch with the newer cuisine. To me, one goes to experience and learn about the old. "New" is everywhere and has no charm for me.

I had looked forward to sitting at the Carousel Bar at our hotel, which in the past hosted famous writers and elegantly dressed people engaged in deep conversation and creative thought. It now hosted noisy, casually dressed tourists engaged in loud, silly conversations – served by blank eyed, unsmiling bartenders, while a jazz band played to people who barely listened. It made me sad.

I did love the Mardi Gras mask shop. I lingered there among its fancifulness, trying to decide which one I would pick to wear to a ball. Who could I be for one magical Cinderella night filled with feathers, lace, rhinestones, velvet, and brocade?

It reminded me of a trip my mother and I took when I was seven years old to a German theater costume room. I will never forget my imagining as I pulled out beautiful garments worn on stage for plays like the Magic Flute or Carmen, or many others. The smell of the room was intoxicating. And while my mother found nothing she liked for her party, I would have gathered them all in my arms and taken them home.

I am such a romantic trapped in this world's reality. Oh,

but a brief moment to dream. But then to walk back out into the street of musical chaos, dancing, and strange people mixed in with a drunk, noisy vacationing crowd. It was a relief to close the hotel door at night and sink back into the quiet and sereneness of a room filled with graciousness and peace and find the comfort of John's embracing arms.

Do not misunderstand me. I do love New Orleans, but I appreciate the spirit of what it once probably was, more than what it had become. But that is just me.

CHAPTER THREE
THE DISCOVERY

Business wise it has been a disappointment for John, but he gave in to my plea to not return home yet. So, we headed along the coast to Savannah.

What a beautiful city. All the old has been perfectly preserved. I floated from one garden spot to the next in absolute bliss. I asked John to please buy the whole city for me. I got the "that's so not going to happen look." I cannot describe my feelings for this place.

I saw a few 'others' but I could not focus on them for soaking in all the beauty around me. It wrapped me in a soft, warm blanket and gently rocked my soul.

But three days later it was time to leave. I cried. It was like leaving a part of me behind that I did not know existed before. Oh well, we must return home and I must face the reality of being a wife and create a home for the two of us. So, we packed the car and set out for home using the back roads only. And that was destiny's path forward.

We had driven a couple of hours when I cried out for John to stop the car. Something in my voice caused him to unquestionably do that. What caused my excitement was a 'For Sale' sign at the entrance to a road lined with beautiful moss-covered trees. John reminded me that we were not looking to buy land, but I begged him to let me see what was down the overgrown dirt road. His look told me I was crazy, but he agreed as long as he could stay in the car and check his emails. That was agreeable to me, so I left the car and started my journey down the dirt road.

About half a mile in I saw a chimney and the remains of what once was a very large house. There were rose bushes, iris, and small trees in what once was probably a beautiful garden area, now struck down by neglect but still stubborn enough to try and catch the notice of someone who cared.

I walked around the shell of the house. There was a set of marble steps at the front that led upwards to nowhere except to a view of rubble. It made me sad. Who had lived here? What happened? Why hasn't anyone done something with this place?

I walked on and found myself at the edge of a river. To my right and left were overgrown fields. As I stood there gazing at the lazy moving water, I heard singing and rustling of grass to my right. Then, to my amazement I saw a large group of Black people dressed in colorful clothing, the women carrying baskets of cotton on their heads, small children ran joyfully in front of them.

As they came closer, the whole landscape changed, and I was suddenly on the property of a grand plantation. I looked back and saw the great house in all its magnificence. I also saw small cabins way off to the side.

As the group grew closer, I was surrounded and swept along toward their homes. One older grey-haired man asked who I was and introduced himself as Silas. "I'm Elizabeth" I answered. "I hope I'm not intruding here, but I saw the for-sale sign on the road and came to see what was here."

''Oh yes,'' sighed Silas, "the sign. We do have people occasionally wander through here, but you are the first to be aware of our presence. Are you afraid?" "Absolutely not, should I be?" I inquired. Silas laughed heartily. I felt very accepted by these 'others'.

"Come with us, it is almost supper time. You can join us if you do not mind a simple meal." "I would love that," I squealed, almost sounding like a small child offered a piece of candy.

We walked to the small cabins. Couples peeled off with their children to their own homes, and Silas led me to his. He told me his wife had died young of a fever and he had never remarried for fear of being separated from someone he cared about again. Somehow, he had become the patriarch of the group. He said the older women of the group often bickered as to who would be the one to bring him supper. He smiled with a twinkle in his old, tired eyes and just as he said that, two women showed up with our supper, flirting and laughing as they served us. We sat outside and ate beans, rice, and cornbread. So good that it rivaled all I had tasted on my trip so far.

As we ate, the sun began to set and a cool breeze swept gently in, so Silas made a small fire for us to sit by. A group of the others came and sat with us. Several children played around us; their laughter carried on the soft, cool breeze. Fireflies began to twinkle, and the little ones chased madly after them.

"Tell me about your life here, if you don't mind?" I asked. Silas sat back in his rocking chair, pulled out a pipe and looked in the direction of the big house. A sad look came over his wrinkled, wise face.

"Well, all of us were either purchased at a market in Charleston or born here. A man and his wife bought us, but she was the one who picked. She went around speaking to all the slaves, inquiring about their skills, and if they had children with them. When the auction started, she whispered to her husband who to bid on. They bought about 40 of us that day. For some reason she let married couples stay together and their children were included in the sale. She once told me that she knew that a woman could lose her mate and survive, but if her children were taken from her and she did not know what happened to them, it could cause a woman to die inside. So, it seemed best on a practical level to keep them together. She said this with such conviction I often wondered if she knew this from personal circumstances. When I saw the looks of relief and gratefulness in the purchased women's faces, I knew she was right. She earned their undying faithfulness to her that day."

"Olivia was her name," Silas continued. "We learned that she was from someplace up north. The master's name was Henry, and apparently (and this is hearsay) he was a young southern gentleman of meager income but desired to own his own plantation and fit into the higher southern society."

"He traveled to New York where he met Olivia, they married and returned here to this piece of land left to him by his grandfather. He built the house for Olivia, and they decided cotton would be their crop. Hence, he needed workers, and money seemed to be an issue no longer."

"Seeing as how it seemed to be Olivia's money, it was an arrangement that let Olivia decide how things would be run. She had the slave quarters built before they went to Charleston, so when we arrived here, we had a lovely place to live. We soon learned that was not the case of the surrounding plantations."

"She and Henry never had children. Not sure why. And even though we knew who was in charge, she never let Henry's peers be aware of it. When she would host dinners for his friends and their wives, she made sure that Henry looked the important man he was supposed to be. And all of us knew our part. Olivia would come down here and ask the younger boys who would like to work the night pulling the rope fan over the dinner table. They all wanted to do it because they knew she would fill the chosen one's pockets with penny candy at evenings end. They would happily sit and pull that rope for hours!"

"She made sure that when Henry rode through the fields with his friends that he would look like the hardened plantation owner. Before we ever arrived here, he had hired two overseers to ride the fields and make sure everyone did their work. One day soon after we had arrived and started working, one of the men took a whip to one of the women. He disappeared that very night. Rumor had it that Olivia cut his throat in the middle of the night; however, no body was ever found and no questions were ever asked. A new man was hired the next day. He carried a rifle and whip but never used them except when Henry and his friends rode through. One of the overseers would shoot his rifle off to kill a snake, rat, or bird. Naturally one of the women would scream at the sudden shot and Henry would nod his approval at the guard and smile at his friends who nodded their approval of his keeping the slaves in line."

"Olivia was a genius landowner. She took care of the books and sale of the cotton and provided us with food and clothing too. Henry stayed out of her way and let her do it all while he received the honors. The bonus for him was to spend his time flaunting his money and indulging in affairs when away on trips. But they both seemed happy with the arrangement."

"Sara, over there," he said, pointing at a pretty, young woman, "was the family cook. Olivia taught her southern dishes, but Sara developed a style of her own using different herbs and spices. Guests would rave about her food. Husbands would flirt openly with her and try to buy her away for themselves. At the table one night, one of Henry's best friends asked him if he had had his way with Sara. Right in front of Olivia! And Henry just smiled slyly and said,' of course. She is a good girl' and winked at her. Olivia just looked down at her hands with a fake hurt look on her face. The men roared with laughter, while their wives gave Olivia a sympathetic look. But Olivia knew this was all part of the game and we all knew Henry had never touched Sara or any of the young girls on the plantation."

"We only saw Missus Olivia upset and angry one time. She came flying on her horse down to the fields, jumped off near where one of the older boys was working. Thomas, he was a good worker about 16 or 17 years old.

We could not hear what she was saying but her arms were flailing, and she was stamping her feet. What a sight. We all stood there in disbelief, then she got on her horse and rode furiously back to the big house. That night and for a week after Thomas was quiet. Shied away from everyone, slept down by the river at night. We were terrified he had done something bad like stealing or worse."

"A week later, here comes Olivia in a wagon to Thomas' parents' house. Beside her was a young, pretty slave girl we recognized from town. Anyway, Olivia helped her off the wagon and at once we could see that she was early on with child and obviously had been repeatedly punished for her transgression. Her name was Rebecca and when she saw Thomas and he saw her, they ran together both weeping so hard I thought they both would collapse and die."

"That next Sunday, they jumped the broom. We raised them their own cabin. Thomas continued working the cotton and Rebecca worked at the big house. She had a knack for sewing, so Olivia had Henry buy bolts of fabric when he went to Savannah and Rebecca made Olivia's fancy dresses and clothes for us too."

"Olivia was miffed at Thomas for a long time. It had taken a lot of bargaining and a lot more money and exchange of favors to buy Rebecca for Thomas. But when that baby was born, seemed her anger toward him disappeared. He was a devoted father and little Annie was the first baby born here. She was a funny little girl. Always kept Olivia laughing at her antics. Henry was even fond of her. She would toddle over to his chair and demand candy. Henry would stare at her real mean like, and she would put her hands on her hips and stare mean right back. Finally, and always, Henry would break into laughter and hand her a piece of wrapped chocolate which magically always seemed to be in his pocket. That is Annie over there." Annie waved at me and smiled.

"Did anyone ever try to run away?" I asked. "Would you?" replied Silas. "Knowing you were safe here and treated like humans. We knew what horrors went on elsewhere. We were blessed to be here. Olivia loved us and we prayed she would not ever die before Henry. He was a good man of sorts but left on his own he would probably have turned on us to keep face with his friends. That first year we did have one of the men escape. Left his family behind thinking he would come back for them, perhaps. Not a week later we heard he had been found and shot. I never could shake the feeling that Henry's dark side was involved somehow."

"Yes, Olivia loved us, and we were loyal to her until death. Martha over there had a baby once and almost died. Olivia brought in a doctor and stayed by her side until she recovered. Took care of that baby like it was her own. Sometimes when Henry was away, she would come and spend the entire day playing with the children so they would not have to work in the fields picking cotton. She even taught them to read and write. I do not think Henry ever knew about that."

"And on Sunday we were blessed to have a preacher come by. Olivia would come down and attend service with us. She loved the hymns and would clap and dance with us. I know for sure that she is in heaven, still watching over us."

"The day the government set us free, she came to each one of us with freedman papers and encouraged us to go. She and Henry were old and sickly. There was no heir. Most of us nodded no and stayed. A few young ones took off to see the world."

"We stayed until they both died. Henry went first, heart attack, I think. There was a huge funeral. Hundreds came to pay their respects. But when Olivia died, no one came or cared. She never had friends of her own. She had given her life to us. We gave her a right proper funeral with flowers from her garden. Seth, over there, made a beautiful wooden cross and placed it next to Henrys' huge monument in the family plot. I say family, but it was just the two of them. There was a special area reserved for us elsewhere. Sara cooked up all Olivia's favorite food and we celebrated her life for two days. We had no idea what to do or where to go, but a week after that a fever spread through our small plantation and that was that. Problem solved."

“We have watched the house fall to ruin over time. The weeds and brush covering up our lives. But we were happy here.”

“So, why have you stayed here? Why not move on? You could see her again.” I inquired. “I don’t know,” sighed Silas. When we leave for good, who will know our story. Olivia’s goodness will never be known. Don’t seem right.’’

“But I know now. I will write your story. People will come to love Olivia and all of you like I have now! You are all buried on this property, right? I will find the graves and mark them. I will clean the place up and make the gardens beautiful again. Your names will be known. I will speak them out. It is time for you to go.”

Silas sat silently for a while, rocking, and smoking his pipe. “You know, you are right. Come on everyone. You too, Elizabeth. Get the drum and the banjo. Put on your best clothes. We are going home. Let's go see Jesus and Olivia!”

And just like that, a long line of people sang and danced down to the water’s edge. A fire was built, and the ‘others’ slowly faded into the fire’s shadows. They danced happily into the lazy river. The sweet rhythmic music slowly faded to reveal only the sounds of cicadas, crickets, and the sound of water lapping on the bank. I watched and cried happily for them.

Suddenly, I felt John at my side. The darkness of night slipped away, and it was bright afternoon again. “You have been gone an hour. I was getting worried. What have you been doing?” I looked at him with happy tears and said,” I have been dancing with the ghosts!”

CHAPTER FOUR
SIX YEARS LATER

I have kept my promise to Silas. John purchased the land. And I did extensive research on it. Amazingly enough I found a picture of the original house and enough information to confirm Silas' story. We have built our home on the original site incorporating the lovely marble stairs. I have restored the gardens, located all the graves, marked them to the best of my ability and fenced in the plots. We are building new cabins near the river in hopes of turning the place into a Bed & Breakfast. We call our new home Olivia's Plantation.

Every year on the date I met Silas and the others, I go to the riverbank at nightfall. My daughter Sara goes with me. We build a fire and place a basket of roses and iris from the garden into the water and watch it miraculously float across to the other side, ignoring the currant, and then disappearing. I believe somehow it is plucked from the water and is delivered to Olivia. Sara and I take turns reading the names that I found registered to this land. Henry, Olivia, Silas, Seth, Sara, Martha, Thomas, Rebecca, Annie, and so many others. And I remember their shadows, dancing into the river. And Sara and I dance together in the shallow water's edge to honor them.

Rest in peace and joy, my friends.

The End

ABOUT THE AUTHOR

Nancy is an only child who spent most of her childhood in Germany where she and her parents traveled extensively whenever possible. At one point they were stationed close to the Black Forest, and they would have picnics on the soft green moss under tall, sun-streamed trees. Visiting castles was her favorite thing to do. All of this helped form her imaginings at an early age and has recently been expressed in her newfound pastime of writing. She has realized her writing always seems to have a thread of some kind of bittersweet aloneness, which she herself has come to embrace in her later years.

www.ingramcontent.com/pod-product-compliance
Lightning Source LLC
LaVergne TN
LVHW052113160826
845678LV00015B/3524

* 9 7 9 8 7 9 8 6 0 9 7 4 1 *